The story so far...

Ella Devonshire is one of those girls that just seem to have it all: looks, intelligence, great mates, boyfriends and, as if that weren't enough, she also has Mysti, a fairy sent to guide and watch over her. Mysti has helped Ella out of a few scrapes and saved the day more than once and now Ella is glad to have her around. But there's something happening to Mysti; she's fallen in love with human boy Rick and maybe everything isn't quite as it seems.

Ella xx

Mysti x

The complicated bit is why I've fallen out of love with Thorn and in love with Rick. Solve that one and you'd make world peace look easy.

Oh, Pease. You just don't get it.

OK, so Thorn is a gorgeous hunky fairy dreamboat that your mother approves of... and Rick is a big clumsy human that... That's it! There's no contest.

Thorn/Rick pros and cons...

Thorn Oakwood

Category: Fairy
Height: 3 cm
Hair: Flaxen
Age: 300
Hobbies: Mouse racing, Acorn throwing
PROs: Mother approves
CONs: None. That's the problem

Rick Taylor

Category: Human
Height: 5' 10"
Hair: Brown
Age: 16
Hobbies: Music, Footie
PROs: None. That's the attraction
CONs: Doesn't believe in fairies

7

11

The Heath...

16

You're quiet... Are you alright?

No, I'm not alright. Now Thorn has the same hair colour as Rick I'm more confused than ever. I'm going home.

Goldrush Hall...

Mysti... please don't slam the leaf like that.

Mysti?

I thought I was in love with Thorn but then I met Rick and he's a human and I know I shouldn't have feelings for a human but I do and now I don't think I'm in love with Thorn anymore... except that I hate it when he talks to Pease and... so maybe I am... but I can't stop thinking about Rick and...

There's more?

You'd think that was enough, but Thorn has made his hair the same colour as Rick's so it's even more confusing. And now Pease is GRUMPY.

i Grumpy

Not one of the seven dwarves. She means cantankerous, crabby, cranky. But then you've never been like that, have you?

20

"You were a delight on the pianoforte, Miss Rainbowfrost."

"And enchanting at the ball."

No, Mysti. That human boy... he was your father.

"It is a truth universally acknowledged, that a single man in possession of a good fortune, must be in want of a wife."

So... who am I?

Why, you're the same person you were when you woke up this morning... Mysti Rainbowfrost...

Then why do I feel like I don't know who I am anymore...

I'm sorry. I thought knowing about your father would help. It explains why you're so drawn to the human world.

But I thought that was because I was cool and rebellious... not because I was genetically programmed to be like that. It makes a nonsense of my whole life.

27

31

We get the holiday we wanted... with no parents.
But with Mr. Mills... he's bound to make it fun.
Plenty of hunky, fit expedition-type guys...
Phwoarr!!

34

After you'd gone, Thorn came back and asked me if I'd like to go mouse racing...

Mysti! Your eyes - what's the matter?

JEALOUSY. I hate the thought of Thorn asking you out.

i Jealousy

According to Shakespeare, "the green eyed monster". Lousy. Really lousy. At least when you were two years old you could throw yourself on the floor and kick and scream. Now this wonderful human emotion ties you in knots and you have to smile sweetly and pretend. "Jealous? Moi? You have got to be kidding." AKA denial.

Huh? But you love Rick.

Doesn't matter.

That's not fair... Suppose I'll have to feel grumpy again...

Hang on... let me think. We can't go through that again.

41

42

43

So, the Elephant is going on the trip and you stay behind..?

Yes... because -

Quiet! The Elephant goes away with other boys... How, precisely, does that help you to trap her?

But you don't understand, father...

Don't you contradict me, son! I understand perfectly well that my son has failed again.

If I could just explain...

Go on...

I have learnt much of their world and camping just isn't cool... it's what they call "sad".

45

What is wrong with everyone? It's like they've had new personalities implanted to confuse me.

Oh there you are...

Like you **care**...

I was worried about you.

Well don't be. It's no big deal. I just have no idea who I am any more.

Tatiana... you're being too hard on yourself...

But maybe I should have told her before...

There are no shoulds or oughts, Tatiana, that is human nonsense. All you have to deal with is what happens now.

Tatiana, for now she's confused, upset. But when she's ready she'll need you. She'll have many questions.

Exactly. Mysti is furious with me and has flown off in a rage... Who knows what will happen...

56

So you see, since there was no way we could make a life together –

You never told him?

It was for the best, Mysti. But he was a good, kind human and he would have been very proud of you.

10 pink handbags there for me to buy, 10 pink handbags there fo
10 pink handbags there for me to buy, 10 pink
BEEP IF YOU FANCY ORLANDO BLOOM!!
But if 1 pink handbag should accidently fly, there'd be 9 pink handbags there for me bu

Dad returns with Ella's vital equipment...

Hgnnnnnnnnnn!!!

Ugnnnnnnnhhh!!!

God, what has Ella got in here?

Hooray... scabby Abby's in her room, smelly Ella's away... I get QUALITY TIME.

i Quality time

In Jack's case, a chance to thrash the pants off someone by cheating at a board game.

In dad's case, an attempt to bond with the son he is increasingly convinced has been swapped by aliens as part of a bizarre intergalactic experiment.

61

I was your age once

All parents say this, but it was so long ago that it's hardly relevant. What have penny farthings, gramophones and hand knitted socks got to do with the angst you're going through today?

69

73

Oh, Thorn, this is wonderful...

Yes, it's a shame Mysti couldn't come too...

Mysti?

That evening...

You're the sad one.

Are you OK?

Yeah... Can't see what I ever saw in him.

85

101

So I'm the new golden girl around here: sympathy for the sore ankle; excused from chores; dad is really pleased with my report; and Abby and Jack have annoyed mum and dad while I was away, meaning even more Brownie points for me!

So, is this the all new Ella?

Not exactly. I mean, who wants to be good? But I might make the most of it for a while.

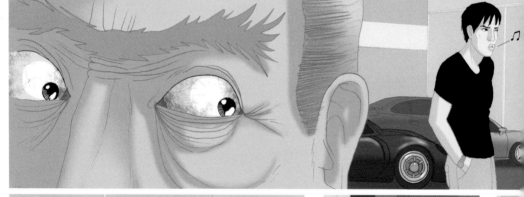

104

No! He's a teacher and... A crush is sort of like fancying someone when you shouldn't.

I don't think anyone's ever had a crush on Professor Dust!

He's just the best teacher - history is my favourite subject!

Hang on... sounds like you're turning into Miss Perfect. What are you going to need me for?

111

112

In Episode 5...

Mysti comes up with a magical scheme to meet her father, but it doesn't go quite as planned...

Find out what happens when Ska gets arrested; is it going to be enough to stop the Drow's evil plot?

All my adventures are now available to buy from my website

www.mysti.co.uk/shop